The Withering Palace

(A Dark Faerie Tale #0.1)

Alexia Purdy

The Withering Palace
(A Dark Faerie Tale Novella #0.1)
Copyright © April 2014 by Alexia Purdy
All rights reserved

Lyrical Lit. Publishing
P.O. Box 33104
Las Vegas, NV 89128

This book is dedicated to Josh

Thank you for showing me that it's worth it.

Untold darkness rules the Unseelie realm of the Land of Faerie. Hidden in this vast area, Aveta, the future queen of the Unseelie Army perfects her gifts over lifetimes. Learning that magic isn't the only way to manipulate the world around her, this naive girl grows into a woman of strength and cunning, ultimately becoming one of the most feared leaders in Faerie.

Underneath her hardened exterior, lies a woman who has known the darkest of hearts, the agony of love, the pull of the consuming power coursing through her veins and what it takes to be ruler of the Unseelie within the walls of The Withering Palace.

Table of Contents

"You will never be queen, for I will live forever…"

Chapter One

The slugs were moving slow and determined across the masonry and past the overly treaded path of the Unseelie Sluagh. Aveta kept to the walls to keep such lowly beings company, blending into the darkness the niches offered as she watched the gruesome parade of soldiers step past. The walkway shook under their practiced unified beat and with the massive amounts of bodies floating by. They never noticed her or were told to ignore her anyway. It was how she liked it though. For the Unseelie Princess found it easier to disappear into the tiny cracks than to be reprimanded by the unforgiving ruling Queen, her mother, for interrupting.

Today, the army was preparing to head out to and run down the nearby territories. It was a given that Queen Elisandra had become obsessed with obtaining more ground, more slaves and more of Faerie than the boundaries of the East where The Withering Palace, their home, could be found. Aveta rarely saw anything outside the walls of the palace, kept secluded and out of the reach of anything beyond this place. It made her curiosity flare up each time she saw them pour out of the exits of the castle, and disappear in legions into the surrounding forest.

Days would pass before they'd return, either beaten or war torn from fierce battles that took heavy losses on both sides. The Unseelie soldiers, Faery and Sluagh alike would drag themselves back into the sanctuary of The Withering Palace, bleeding, dying or already gone, lost to the world or turning to dust as the land withdrew the magic that animated them. She'd watched battalion after battalion trudge back in, collapsing all over the place while hundreds of servants ran amuck to try and heal all the injured, the lost. It would be weeks before another battle could ensue, but it would happen again, and again.

The Queen was never satisfied.

Chapter Two

"Never show them fear." Her mother's stern voice drilled into her head like a constant hum, vibrating her eye sockets to the point of unending pain. She'd been standing straight holding out the Queen's staff and orb of the Unseeing, one in each hand. Her arms were wavering, shaking under the strain as her tears streamed down her flushed cheeks. It'd been what felt like hours, maybe just one, but the prickling pain enveloping her arms and shoulders no longer felt real to her. It came, took another little bit of her beaten heart and slammed it to the ground.

These were the punishments for not living up to expectations. This was the payment required to continue on in the day when the Queen was upset and disappointed in all who served her. Elisandra was pure wickedness on these sorts of morns and Aveta usually was well versed in avoiding her at all costs. Not this day though. She'd had the misfortune of becoming the focus of her mother's wrath after her father, King Seritus, the Queen's First lieutenant, had argued with Elisandra about something or another. Aveta was never privy to their conversations, only to the torturous downpour of malice formed inside the Queen's insanity from the confrontation.

"You pathetic runt. You shake like a wilted flower, dripping your britches with foul smelling stench." The queen shook her head before snatching her jeweled staff and orb out of Aveta's clutches. She fingered the long, bejeweled symbol of power, her thin, delicate fingers lovingly stroking the rubies and emeralds strewn throughout the flashy staff.

Aveta didn't dare move, but did let her weak, tingling arms lower to her sides. She could barely feel them, the fiery, screaming pain long gone from them, replaced with a numbness that equaled the one in her heart. No longer crying, her tears had ceased to flow, replaced with nothing but hate and loathing.

"A pity you will never be Queen, for I will rule forever." Her mother's hot breath whistled past her ear before the cold woman twirled and swished her long skirts out of the room.

Aveta lets out the sob she she'd been holding, collapsing to the floor in pure exhaustion. It wasn't even noon and her body begged for release. Her caretaker, Eladril rushed to her side, wiping her face as she pulled her into her warm chest, holding her slack weight with her strong and well used muscles.

"Aveta, wake up. You mustn't let it overtake you, this darkness. Here." A cool rim touched Aveta's lips and sloshed even colder fluid into her mouth. She gave a sputtering cough before she was able to control the liquid, letting it slide down her throat and into her core. The soothing draught worked quickly, reviving her into her previously alert self. The tingle in her strained arms dissipated as the blood returned into them, rushing to warm her frigid finger tips.

"Let me die." She turned away from Eladril, wanting to sink into the stone, silently praying to the walls to take her in and encase her in the infinite, cold stone. At least the stone could not feel pain, could not bleed, and could not have its soul crushed to oblivion.

Take me, please, hide me in your cool embrace... she whispered to the dusty floor.

"Hush, now child. There be none of that." Eladril stood and dragged the girl to her feet, giving her a good jolting shake. "Get on your feet. You should be all right now, but do stay out of the Queen's sight for the next few days if you can. I fear it won't be long before she goes much too far with your fragile life." She hugged Aveta and turned, grabbing the girl's clammy hand and tugged gently, coercing her to follow. "Come."

Aveta said nothing. In fact, she did nothing to acknowledge her surroundings or the murmur of voices hissing all around her. She paid no mind to anyone as they crossed past rows of soldiers, snickering at her and her handmaiden. Eladril kept her grip firm as she continued to drag her on and on, to who knows where. Aveta did not care anymore.

"Almost there," The handmaiden tugged continually, squeezing Aveta's fingers enough to bring her out of the fog she'd pulled taut about her. The girl stared ahead, the tears long smeared away but the tiny salt still clung to her skin. It felt dry, caked on and irritated her delicate skin. Only now, with the annoying sensation did she bother to peek about, noticing that they were deeper into the castle dungeons than she's ever been before.

"Where are we?" Her voice sounded foreign, cold and disconnected.

"A place to hide, whenever you need to."

She lifted an eyebrow to Eladril, her interest invested in such a mystery presented. What did the woman mean? What sort of hidden place could remain in this vast castle? Her curiosity peaked as they passed the dungeons into slim crevices that lined the walls and made it near impossible for Eladril to slip through. Aveta had no problem squeezing through the fissures, but the darkness creeping over them as the light became more and more suffocated by the darkness gripped her with fear.

"Is it much farther?" Aveta's lips trembled, the cool breeze shifting through the underground made her wonder if there was an exit nearby.

"No, not much. Here," Eladril stopped, kneeling down to Aveta's level, holding out a small stone. It flared to life as the woman whispered over it and she cupped it into the girl's tiny hands. "This will light the rest of the way for you. I'll go through this once with you, and only once. I can never enter again after that, it has drained too much of my entity."

Aveta furrowed her brows, confused. "What do you mean?"

Eladril rubbed her forehead and peered over her shoulder. "The labyrinth. It's the last part of the dungeon. I heard your mother was going to place you here soon, in hopes that you won't make it out. I've been here before, I know how to get in and out and that was to save my brother from certain death. The Labyrinth is as alive as the Withering Palace. The castle likes you though, a great advantage for its future queen. Do you hear it speak to you?"

Aveta nodded, thinking about the frequent whispers from the walls which had plagued her since she could remember. They would speak warnings, which at first she'd ignored, but now, she knew better. It was the castle's warnings of danger and whispering secrets to her. She'd often wondered if her mother heard the palace as she did. To this day, her mother had never given an indication that she had.

"Well, listen to the walls, they'll whisper to you the way to go if you really listen. It helped me get my brother out. The palace chooses those that are pure of heart, pure of power, regardless if we are Unseelie. Your mother hears no such voices. She is not the true ruler." She smiled, smoothed Aveta's raven colored hair back before standing straight again, staring at the leering entrance to the labyrinth.

"What's in there that drains our essence?" Aveta's voice echoed across the slippery stone walls, smoothed over by time, water and slick moss. The labyrinth beyond felt like another world.

"Darkness." Eladril's voice bounced across the cavern walls until the stone absorbed it, leaving only silence and stifling air. "Whatever you see in there, don't look at it. Remember, only you can make it real. I don't see what you'll see, you won't see what I do. It will turn into your worst nightmares, but only you can make it stop."

"What if I do look at it? What happens?"

Eladril lowered her gaze to the ground, paling in the illumination of the witch light. "Look at the darkness enough times and you wither to nothing, or worse….go mad and become one of them."

Aveta swallowed the knot formed in her throat. She tightened her grip around Eladril's fingers, sweat already slicking across both their skins.

"Why do I have to do this?"

Eladril sucked in a breath and moments felt like an eternity before she answered.

"You will be queen one day, and the challenge against your mother will not be easy. You will first match wits, then, if that does not choose a victor, the labyrinth is the second challenge. Whomever makes it through this labyrinth alive, claims the crown."

"Did my mother win that way?"

Eladril's fingers let her go as she kneeled down once more

beside her. "Your mother won in a most treacherous way. Your grandmother was the rightful queen, but Elisandra killed her still. Queen Analise could've chosen her heir, too, which would've been you, eventually. But your mother, in her wicked ways, chose her destiny and damned herself for killing the rightful queen. The palace will never accept her as queen, it will never be rightfully hers. She will never have the full power of it. Only you can do this. You were born to."

She stood once more, lacing her fingers through the young princess' hand.

"What if I'm not strong enough to challenge her and win?" Aveta never felt smaller. Her mother scared her more than the sluagh creatures of her vast army.

"You will. In time, you will be much stronger than you'll ever imagine."

Chapter Three

Stepping into the vast oblivion before them, the walls rose high above, stretching toward the darkened ceiling of the cavern. It disappeared beyond the witchlight, making it feel smaller than it was. Aveta struggled to not pull away from Eladril and run screaming from the monstrosity before them. The length of this leg of the Labyrinth looked endless before it sharply turned and faded into the inky blackness surrounding them.

"Don't look up, they come from all directions. Focus on stepping forward. It's a labyrinth, but it's not a traditional labyrinth. If it tests you long enough and fails, it will drop you out the other side. That's what we need to focus on."

Aveta tilted her chin, biting down on her lip hard as each step crunched against the grit on the cavern floor. Nothing but their sharp, quick breaths could be heard above the silence, and it roared in her ears like a violent funnel. If it was really going to be as bad as Eladril said, she had to gather her wits and strength about her before she shivered her fear into being and her life was sucked away.

No, she wouldn't let that happen, there was no way to fail. It was this or certain death. There was nothing that could make her more determined to not die in this treacherous place. It made her want to live even more.

The first few minutes were maddening more than anything

else. Distant echoes of screeching things and flapping wings made her skin crawl. Only the constant tug from Eladril to keep moving kept her wits intact, though she doubted she could scream if she had to. The sandpaper her throat had morphed into stuck to itself. Even her heart was hammering loudly in her chest, almost drowning out the void of sparse noise before them.

So this is what it felt to drown. If not, it was probably quite close to it. Even though they were immortal, faeries could still die from such mundane tragedies. Aveta preferred to never have to experience such a thing as dying. One day maybe, years from now, when time had left her bitter and cold, maybe then would she embrace the sweet arms of death. Until then, she'd make it through. There was no other choice.

"Aveta…," Eladril's voice cut off as they turned down the first bend and stood face to face with two figures at the other end. They were wrapped in darkness, which was all they could tell from the distance. Still, as they walked forward, the two figures, one shorter than the other matched their pace and continued towards them at an equal stance.

"I know, don't look at them."

She could feel Eladril's fear leak across her skin. The woman may have just been a handmaiden to the royal family, but she was an Empath, and had traits of an oracle, a faery gifted with telepathy, precognitive abilities and healing magic. She wasn't strong enough to be considered special and under the Queen's direct counsel, but she was gifted enough to be placed on the princess' guard and servitude. Eladril's long, brown hair was tied back in a twisted braid, weaved with intricate knots for it was so long. It complimented her creamy complexion well. Aveta hoped her long, black hair would be just as beautiful against her pale skin when she grew older. Though she considered herself beautiful, she didn't believe that her beauty would ever match that of her mother's or Eladril's.

The figures were just feet from them and the closer they approached, the colder the cavern air became. The stench of death filled Aveta's nostrils, gagging her on the choking fumes.

Don't look at them, follow the ground, the dirt… the snakes?

She gasped, no longer worried about the figures, who were now gone from sight while the ground was moving in slithering, shiny coils. She gripped Eladril's hand as she stepped on one, feeling its body jerk under her boot, but she refused to look down again. The darkness ahead was all she could take as her eyes peeled wide open, half immersed in the witchlight shaking in Eladril's palm and the closing dark.

I can do this, I can do this.

She wasn't feeling positive as the words swirled about in her head. She felt the snakes coiling around her ankles, taking all she had to not kick at them.

"Eladril?" The older faery seemed more grounded than Aveta, even though from their contact, the child could feel the growing dread emanating from her guardian. "What's on the other side of the labyrinth?"

The crawling sensation remained for few moments more, until it felt as if the ground had solidified and they were walking along the moist rock once more.

"Well, it's the exit of this cavern. It leads into another place, a safe one. But, there are dangers there too. It's a territory of Faerie, but it's not ruled by the Unseelie or the Seelie courts."

Fascinated, Aveta pressed on for more details. "What do you mean?"

Eladril sucked in a breath, the air turning thicker as they took more turns in the tangle of halls and dead ends they kept running into. There were no imaginary threats here, but the constant turns and disorientation were frightening nonetheless.

"Well, the sky is a constant pink tangerine, like an everlasting sunset. There are trees that grow in Faerie and the human world and things that grow in neither. The poppies are deadly, so stay away from them. Only a few lucky ones are immune, and most live in this part of the land."

"Is it as dangerous as our land?"

"No, but if you're not meant to be there, it will slowly kill you from the poison drifts of poppy vapor."

"How will we survive that?"

Eladril peered down at the girl, her lovely blue eyes crinkling as she smiled. "I know I'm immune, my brother lives there too and has not had any lasting effects. He's safe there. You'll know if it's toxic to you, soon enough. If not, you won't feel any different."

The thought made her skin crawl, but Aveta pressed on,

following Eladril around another corner where the path led up into steps carved out of stone into a dark, black hole, big enough for just one of them to crawl through at a time.

"Eladril?" Aveta peered over to her guardian, fear ebbing into her shiny dark eyes.

"Here," Eladril slipped the witchlight into Aveta's tiny palm and curled her fingers around them. "You take this, I have another. If we get separated, keep going. Don't try to find me, I'll get there."

Aveta nodded, bleary eyed as the tears stung behind her lids. She didn't want to let go of Eladril. The sickening feeling filling her up as she watched the woman step up the stairs ahead of her made her wonder if they would be separated. It was a small comfort that she'd told her that she'd made it through here and back before, but it was only just.

Now that Eladril was several steps ahead, the lonely darkness behind her made her feel more exposed and she hurried up behind her guardian. As the hole swallowed Eladril, she no longer could hear the woman shuffling as her dresses brushed against the stone. Aveta gulped down the bile rising to her throat as she took the first crawling steps into the nothingness ahead. It was hard to crawl with the witchlight in hand, and hold the tiny stone high enough to see ahead.

It didn't matter though because once the last of her body made it into the tight space, the witchlight extinguished with one rushed gust of air.

She paused, wondering what dark magic had done such a thing. There was no up or down and the light had vanquished from behind her too. There was nothing, just black, inky darkness. Tentatively, she pressed forward, feeling her way through the slick, grimy rock and what felt like tendrils of underground foliage snaking their way down the walls and grabbing onto her hair as if it had fingers.

Aveta…

She gasped, hearing a voice whispering across her face. It was so close she could almost feel the air move by her nose. What if it was something dreadful? The unknown was even more terrifying without light and Aveta struggled to keep her hands and knees inching forward.

Aveta…

It got even closer, and louder by her ear. She swatted at her side like there was a buzzing fly next to her.

No! Don't acknowledge it! You'll give it more power… Eladril's words echoed in her mind and she gritted her teeth, closing her eyes to feel more with her senses.

Eladril, where are you?

Aveta!

"Eladril?" It was her guardian's scream that made her almost fall forward, catching her muddy dress under her knees. What had her? Where was she?

Help me!

"Eladril!" It couldn't be, the woman's screeches paralyzed her as her breaths sped out of control, and her palms and knees becoming raw from crawling forward as fast as she could. The stone was hard against her skin and stabbed at her joints and palms with each excruciating moment that passed.

Help me!

Aveta fell forward, tumbling down another set of stairs, knocking her head and arms as she rolled down them, landing in a pile of dirty leaves and squishy mud. The voice had startled her and all she could do was lay there in the filth of old water mixed in whatever grit had sat in the puddle she now laid in. The stench was worse, like a pit of death and stale air. She gasped to catch her breath and stared up at the…night sky?

There were stars above, swirling across the sky, twinkling like distant lighthouses, flashing their marked safety, calling her to their embrace.

No, they aren't real. There were no formations in this sky like the ones she'd studied over and over on the endless nights she'd spend out on her balcony, counting the falling stars as they slit the sky with their fires. This was a mirage with star formations she'd never laid eyes upon.

Still, with their enticing twinkles and soft aurora lights off to her right beckoning her to lay there forever, and absorb the beauty, she felt the fatigue and ache of the day's torture overcoming her now, like a weary drug, ready to overtake her consciousness. It would be so easy to just close her eyes and sleep.

Chapter Four

*N*o, *must get up, must keep going…*the poppy fields waited, they called to her, to a place where there was an endless sunset and the trees dangled cherry blossoms down to tangle into her obsidian strands. A safe place, a sanctuary not even her mother could touch.

She pulled her body out of the muck, first her arms to turn her over and then willed her slack legs to inch forward, slipping from the grip of the dead leaves and clinging mud. Her limbs protested every pull and strain, begging for release from the endless torment plaguing her body.

Once free from the puddle, her mind cleared up enough for her to peer about. The constant emptiness, which hovered in the air, somehow made it easier to breathe now, but the endless dark was still overbearing. She'd lost the witchlight in the muck. Eladril was gone, probably having gone through a similar trance. She was sure the woman had broken free much faster than Aveta, but she hoped she hadn't left her behind.

What now? Aveta struggled to her feet, cold and wet, her dress in tatters as she stepped forward. There was nothing but dark, black inky death waiting ahead. Pushing her stringy strands of hair back, she focused as she reined in her fear and swallowed it down. She needed another witchlight, they weren't hard to make. Reaching down, she felt around on the gritty floor before finding a suitable loose stone and gripped it tight in her palm.

She pressed her hands together, closing her eyes as she

infused her magic into the rock. Eladril had shown her this very lesson but a week ago, and Aveta's gratitude for it was beyond measure. She pressed her skin against the stone until it ached, and it dug in, probably drawing a tiny slip of blood. She didn't care. The light was vital in this vacuum of life.

Peering down to sneak a look through the crack of her palms, she saw it softly glowing.

"Brighter." She whispered to it and it pulsated softly, as if struggling to do her bidding. "Come, on, more light!" Her voice was soft, but it echoed loudly against the cavern walls, amplifying it enough to send shivers down her spine. Almost reluctantly, maybe because it was a stone of the darkness, the rock obeyed and shone brighter, making her look away before her night vision was affected by the light.

She grinned down at her twinkling prize, not noticing the approaching figure. As it approached into the circle of light the stone created, Aveta glanced up and gasped, almost dropping her newly formed witchlight.

"Mother?" The form took the shape of the Queen, with matching malicious intents in her dark twinkling eyes.

"You disobeyed me again child." The woman stepped forward, her long swishing skirts brushing the dirty floor of the cavern. Other than the filth clinging to the hem of her dress, she looked pristine, as if she'd been freshly washed and brushed. "You disgusting little tramp. How dare you call yourself my daughter if you run about looking like faery trash?"

Aveta flinched as her mother stalked forward. Was this her greatest fear? Her mother coming to find her and inflicting more endless torment? If that's what it was, and it was only a vision, it should easily go away. Shouldn't it?

She closed her eyes and took in a deep breath, though it became infused with the nose prickling scent of her mother's perfume. Choking on it like a noxious fume, she squeezed her eyes even tighter, willing her mother away.

"You can't make everything disappear. This is the oblivion of your mind. This is who you really are inside. How do you make yourself be gone and still survive? You can't"

"You're not real." Tighter, tighter, keep the eyes closed.

"You know nothing. I never saw anything worth saving in you from the moment of your birth. Your father, he saved you, but

I…I should've done what I wanted to at that exact minute. End your pathetic life."

Don't listen, shut out her words. The tiny voice in Aveta's head morphed into Eladril, and she flung her eyes open, seeing past the Queen to find Eladril watching her quietly ahead.

"Eladril!" She ran forward, aware that she would bump into her mother, but it didn't matter. Her mother wasn't real. Eladril was.

With that, the moment she touched her mother's apparition, it disintegrated into wisps of blackened smoke, screeching as it flew away from them. Could it be so easy to keep the demons at bay? Could they really not hurt them if they knew how to do away with them?

Eladril smiled, arms opened wide as she let the girl fall into her embrace.

"We're almost out of here. Just hang on a bit longer."

"Alright," Aveta found her cheeks wet, doused in salty tears. Maybe this would all end up fine. Maybe she'd learn to walk right through this dreadful place to a safe haven, far from her mother, far from the oppressive life of an Unseelie princess. Somehow, she hoped it would be that way. A place where no one else could follow.

"Come," Eladril tugged on her hand and they walked through more turns, twists and open rooms than they cared to count.

"How much longer until we reach the other side?"

"Not much longer. You've done excellent here. I'm truly impressed that you can handle yourself so well, you're so young." Eladril stepped forward, limping and grimacing. It was only then that Aveta noticed the dark, crimson stain on the side of her dress.

"You're hurt!" Aveta stared wide eyed, fear crawling back into her.

"Yes, child. Don't worry, once we leave here, all will be well."

Aveta wasn't so sure. She gripped her guardian's hand even tighter, feeling the sting of tears flurrying up behind her eyes. She had to keep it together, just a bit longer. It would be okay in the end. Eladril couldn't lie. No faeries could. The land of Faerie forbade it.

"See? Here we are."

In the area ahead, a tiny sliver of light grew as they approached. Soon enough, it was as big as a doorway and Aveta stared into it, hoping to see what lingered on the other side.

"Go on now, I'll be right behind you." Eladril's strained voice made Aveta turn, worry engulfing her as she watched her beloved handmaiden collapse.

"Eladril!" She threw herself on the ground beside her fallen companion. "No! You have to come with me! You have to make it. You said it would be okay."

Eladril smiled, her hand pressed against the wound on her abdomen. It was sticky with dark crimson blood encrusting her fingers. It looked fatal and Aveta swung her eyes from her to the light at the end of the cavern. She could never drag her caretaker that far, she was too heavy for her little seven year old frame.

"Please, get back up. It's not that far. Please…" The girl begged, her tears already dripping to the ground.

"I'm so sorry my dear. I lost concentration. I saw you with your mother and I let the wraith overpower me. I'm so sorry. You can make it. Just go through to the light and all will be fine. It's alright, go."

Aveta shook her head furiously, refusing to believe this was how it was to end. "NO!"

The floor shook as her voice echoed around her and a dusty burst of wind blew her hair back, forcing them both to cover their faces. The groan of rock and falling debris rushed about them, deafening with its roar and vibration.

They had to move now or risk being crushed under the weight of falling rock.

A moment later, the ground ceased to rumble and the dust was left to float about them in calming clouds that settled on the floor, sighing in relief.

"What was that?" Aveta darted her eyes about them, afraid the labyrinth wasn't done with them yet.

Eladril's eyes were focused solely on the girl. Peeled open, fear leaking from them for a moment before she blinked it away and the moment passed. But Aveta had seen it and a deep, aching shame began to flourish with the girl.

"Your powers, they are stronger now."

"Yes," Aveta nodded, sniffing as she wiped her nose and

brushed the tears off her dirty face.

"Can you move things?"

"Yes, the castle moves when I want it to. But I can move small objects without touching them."

"Have you tried to move larger ones?"

Aveta shook her head, the tears starting up again.

Eladril reached out, pushing a loose strand of hair behind Aveta's ear. "Don't cry. You'll be Queen one day. Queens never cry."

Aveta tried her best to stop the outpour, but watching Eladril pale before her eyes only brought on more despair, it choked her spirit inside.

A rub of rocks and sand brought her attention to the approaching figures. Aveta gasped, inching closer to Eladril as they grasped each other tight.

Stone. Pillars of stone were moving toward them, but they had arms and legs and slid along the cavern floor in a scraping loudness. The closer they got, the less they looked like pillars, but had a humanoid shape, rough and rounded with the boulders that made up their heads, arms, torsos and legs, but upright and very much alive.

"What magic is this?" Eladril hissed. Her eyes were wild, though her pallor indicated her time was very near.

Aveta shook her head, staring at the figures who did not approach too close, but hovered around them like a wall of rock. "I…I've seen them in my dreams before…"

Eladril turned toward Aveta, disbelief as understanding flooded her eyes. "You made them. You made them with your mind, didn't you?"

Aveta nodded, afraid of the repercussions of the elemental magic that ran within her veins. Her mother did not possess this power, neither had her father. What did it make of her then?

"It's impossible."

"I used to move little rocks with my mind since I can remember."

"But where is this earthen magic from?"

"I don't know."

Moments passed, each minute taking crimson life from her caretaker.

"Can they help us?" Eladril whispered, her resolve to stay sitting upright waning as time went on.

Aveta peered up at the still stone statues, wondering the same thing. "I—I don't know." Staring at her creations, a new determination bubbled up inside of her, pushing her to make the next move. "Help us. Help me take her to the exit of the cavern there."

The figures moved at her command, dragging their massive bodies across the gritty ground until reaching them. One reached down, shoving its rough arms under Eladril and lifting her as if she weighted nothing. Eladril gripped onto the cold stone, her fingers white from the strain to hold on for dear life. The stone soldier then stood tall and scraped haphazardly along to the very exit of the cavern. They moved with convoluted motion, uneven and almost as if it was laborious to walk, but their massive bodies made it into the entrance and out into the open air.

Aveta stared wide eyed as they marched along, a mere handful, but they appeared scary and enormous to the young girl. That her miniscule magic was capable of such creation, baffled her and she knew she'd have to hide this ability from her mother for certain, or face dire consequences.

They made their way into the light, where a long trail of rich red earth led the rest of the way down the mountain and into a rich field overladen with pink and white poppies swaying in the cool afternoon breeze. The light was delicious on her face and the moment she stepped past the threshold of the cavern, her clothes changed to their previously cleaned and orderly state. With that, she turned to see Eladril climb down from the arms of the stone soldier, also intact and very much alive.

"You did it, Aveta! You made it to the uncharted lands of Faerie!" She pressed forward, joining the young girl with a huge smile. "I knew you could do it."

Aveta gave her a tiny grin, peering at her guardian with nothing but love and gratitude. "I couldn't have done it without you."

"Nonsense. I think you are stronger than you'll ever really know."

"Thank you, Eladril."

"Thank you as well. You saved me with your peculiar magic." Eladril studied the stone guardians, her smile falling ever so slightly. "Never show your mother…or anyone else for that matter. She would kill you if she knew you could do such things."

Aveta nodded. Sadly, the handmaiden was much too correct in that assumption.

"What should I do here?"

Eladril glanced back toward the field of poppies and the wild cherry blossom trees surrounding them. The sky was a burnt orange red and looked peaceful.

"Well, you can do anything you want here. It is sanctuary to you now. Only you know how to get here. You'll be safe here when things go awry and you need to get away from everything."

"Even from mother?"

Eladril sighed, weary and looking fatigued. "Yes, even from your mother."

Chapter Five

The years had carved Aveta's heart into a sharp point that could kill the toughest soldier about. Still, at the age of fifteen, it had not yet been enough to leave her jaded or colder than Queen Elisandra. No, no one could ever be as damaged as the woman who ruled all of the Unseelie court of Faerie.

Aveta smoothed down the cinches in her long, flowing skirt. The tight jeweled bodice made it hard to breath and her rib cage screamed its protest as she straightened to get some air in. Even the snug braids across her head were pulled so taut that her hair was sure to fall out sooner or later. This was the life of a princess and she hated every second of it. The bright colored dress stood out in the gray and black of the servant's dress and that of the soldiers constantly roaming the halls. Still, she kept her chin up, knowing full well she was not to be trifled with.

Today was her coronation to second in command. So young, but she had succeeded in taking all the tests her mother sent her way. There was nothing to do now but to hand the position to her daughter, much to her mother's chagrin. Nothing made Aveta smile more than seeing her mother hesitate when she looked at her now.

No, not even the queen could deny the position of power to a powerful royal. Still, Aveta had to watch her back. Avoiding the Queen was easy enough, she had her field of poppies to disappear into, beyond the labyrinth where no one treads. It'd become not only her sanctuary, but a place of pure solace and peace, a trait she could not find anywhere in the Withering Palace.

Nowhere here?

Aveta turned, hearing the wall's soft whispers as it whined its protests to her for always leaving to the poppy fields.

"Your palace is solace to me, old friend. Just not while under her rule." Her answer was well taken and the walls of the palace quieted down into its normal, quietly whispered banter. Ever since she could remember, it had been a deep comfort to have the walls speak to her. No one else could hear it, no one else knew of the ancient magic controlling the very castle they resided in. Not even Queen Elisandra.

Which was another reason she was being inducted into the position of second in command at such a young age. She knew things others didn't and knew them because the walls had eyes everywhere. Hence the ease of avoiding punishment since that long ago day of torment before Eladril led her into the labyrinth, deep in the gut of the castle and to the poppy fields below. No one would ever touch her again. No one could ever get close enough again.

"Well, I guess I'm as ready as I'll ever be." She smiled at her reflection, knowing how she was already turning into a woman. Her beauty was subtle, but striking. Her long, black as ink strands laid straight over her shoulders and down to the small of her back. Held in place with a thin, diamond encrusted, black-vine metal band, she looked every bit the princess.

This would make her mother's blood boil. Knowing how well loved Aveta was amongst the Unseelie would unhinge her even further. That'd been the plan from the beginning, since the moment she'd emerged from the darkness of the labyrinth with Eladril fussing over her like a mother hen, she'd known that the darkness of the labyrinth had taught her one thing above all else. She would have to strip her enemy of all things precious to them, including her family and her dedicated army. The Withering Palace would be hers for the taking, one day, and Elisandra, her cruel, unloving mother would be no match for her when the time came.

Entering the Royal chambers where mother sat atop her stone dais, the woman's cold stare did nothing to break Aveta's spirit. In fact, she stood straighter and focused her gaze right back at the ruler. This inherently maddened the Queen even further as evidenced by her whitened knuckles as her fingers grasped the edges of the arms of her throne. Her jaw was taut, and her long dark hair hung in long, straight bunches over her shoulders and down her back. Funny how similar they looked, but where Elisandra exuded cold and frigid with hardened black eyes, Aveta was calm, unmoving and so very much alive.

Maybe Elisandra had been alive too long. Her mother was six hundred years old. In all that time, she had no children until Aveta's birth. Whatever the reason for waiting so long was a mystery to her. Maybe it was Aveta's father's wish. Maybe something changed in the woman, but one thing was for certain…Elisandra regretted it with every fiber of her being.

"My daughter." Elisandra stood and held out her hand. Aveta's father, Seritus, stood as well, but did not move from his position to the left of Elisandra. He didn't even so much as meet eyes with Aveta. He'd been so aloof and cold, sometimes Aveta wondered if he'd been mind wiped into submission. It was entirely possible and she relished the fact that she hadn't been tampered with and would never allow herself to become vulnerable enough for Elisandra to do such a thing.

"Mother," Aveta curtsied and ascended up the stone stairs, taking each one slowly as to not trip down the steep aisle. Nothing short of embarrassment for her here and her mother would enjoy every second of it. Nope, she'd never give her a chance to enjoy such a thing.

"Today, she turns fifteen, a young woman, but a ruler none the less. Today, my very flesh and blood becomes anointed as my second in command, Second only to me, Queen Elisandra of the Unseelie Court."

Aveta slipped her fingers into her mother's and squeezed firmly, staring the Queen in the eyes as she let her smile slide across her face. Elisandra returned it, but it was tight and didn't reach her cold eyes. The frigid exchange was nothing uncommon between them, but Elisandra let go first and turned back to sit on her throne.

"You may take the chair to my right now, Princess Aveta."
"Thank you, your Majesty."

*****

Cranston plucked the petals off the poppy, letting it flap softly in the breeze only to let it go as it swirled away into the gusts of wind. Making his way through all the petals, soon all that was left was the wilted stem, which he promptly discarded to pluck another poppy from the ground.

"You're killing them for your amusement?"

"Why not? We crush them when we walk over them all the time." He grinned, his large teeth protruding from his soft lips, white as the clouds on a summer day.

"You're wickedly cruel."

"I litter the world with poppy petals. Could be worse."

Aveta rolled her eyes and laid back onto the soft pillow of flowers beneath them. The poppies grew like weeds like a thick blanket in the field. Though poisonous to most faeries, Aveta and Cranston were immune to its sedative effects. The lovely scent of the flower wafted in and out of her nose as she breathed in the perfumed air. It was light, yet prominent, but it made her relax when this scent came rushing at her whenever she left the cavern exit from the labyrinth.

The labyrinth was nothing to her now. She could walk right through it without a thing bothering her. Eladril never returned to it, but this wasn't her sanctuary, it was Aveta's.

"So your mother was less than pleased about your indoctrination to second in command huh?" He smashed the petals off this poppy, rolling them in his fingers until the sweet scent leaked all over his skin.

"Oh yes. She hates my guts. I enjoy seeing her seethe at me surviving this long."

"When will you challenge her?"

Aveta turned away from staring at his curly, golden brown locks that snarled unruly about his ears and across the back of his neck. Most faery men let their hair grow long and lush. But Cranston was no ordinary Faery man. He was a farm boy, working hard on the fields of this other land of Faerie, toiling much like the humans did to coax the land to bring food and bounty for his family. His mother and siblings depended on his hard work. The soft glow of a tan kept him looking different from other pale faeries. But that was okay with Aveta. She'd loved him from the moment they met, long ago under the cherry blossoms the second time she had come here.

"I don't know."

Cranston turned over, leaning his head on his palm as he handed her a new flower, freshly plucked. "Well don't wait too long; she'll expect it when you're of age. Do it when she thinks she still has time."

Aveta nodded, grinning softly and accepting the cut flower, sad that it would die soon, but happy to receive any gift from Cranston.

Her mother would never accept this boy to marry her only daughter. Their love was never to come to anything, and this fact alone kept Aveta coming back for more.

"I'll know, when the time is right, I'll know."

He grinned at her, letting his fingers tangle in a long strand of her obsidian hair. "I know you will. I just fear for you."

"Don't be afraid. I have so much more power than she's aware of. I'll be fine."

He looked away, staring beyond her in a trance, sadness spilled into his eyes. "I hope so." He let her hair drop and began to draw tiny circles in the dirt. "You can stay here you know. She'll never find you."

Aveta reached out and let her fingers run through his hair. The touch itself sent electric shocks up her arm and made her heart jump. How this ordinary farm boy could make her insides turn to mush was something of a mystery to her.

"I know. But that's not my destiny."

"I wish it were."

Aveta giggled and laid back down on the ground. She wished it were too. How easy would life be here? To indulge in manual labor sounded dreadful, but to have peace and love would make it worth more than anything in Faerie.

"The Withering Palace is mine, I'm destined to claim it from her."

"You don't have to."

"I must."

"But why?"

Yes, why? Why did she have to challenge her mother to the death for the power of a Queen? Deep down inside she felt it, and knew it was what she was meant to do.

"I have to."

With that she sat up, pulling herself to her feet and brushing the dead leaves and dirt from her skirts. "I don't want to talk about it anymore."

Cranston studied her as he pulled the last petal off the barren stem and let the wind suck it into the whirl of air flying about them. "I just wish you could stay here, with me. Be safe and not deal with the treacheries she imposes on you."

"It's not that bad anymore. I think I frighten her now."

"All the more reason to jump ship."

Aveta turned toward her friend, filled with warmth for the young man whom she met that horrid day so long ago. He was her rock, her comfort in this life filled with darkness and pain. Only Cranston understood what she went through, he was the only one who really knew her.

"How 'bout some lunch? I'm practically famished."

Cranston lowered his eyes to the ground knowing full well she just avoided the topic again. The sadness in his face was obvious, but Aveta turned away, not wanting to see it, not wanting to know about any kind of feeling except happiness in this place.

"I caught some fish from the river earlier today. Let's head to my place and we can get that steamed with some rice."

Aveta smiled, watching Cranston stand up to hover over her, holding out his firm hand. She took it and with one quick motion, he had her in his arms. He may only be sixteen, just a year ahead of her, but he was strong, sturdy. Owning a body only a farm boy toiling day in and day out could manage. He swung her around until they were dizzy before he put her back onto her feet. She liked his arms around her, they felt like the safest harbor she could ever find.

They made their way toward his quaint, but cozy home, where his mother would embrace her with a love she had no idea could exist. His siblings were the same, adored her with grins and hugs. She knew it could all disappear one day, but for now, she cherished the hot, cooked lunch, seasoned with love, hope and peace. It was all she needed right now, and it was everything that would keep her sane for the days to come, when it was impossible to visit Cranston, and the nights turned into chilly frost all alone.

Chapter Six

Queen Elisandra watched her daughter ascending from the lower regions of the castle. That girl was up to something and she would discover it sooner or later. As Aveta took another turn down the hall, and headed to her chambers, Elisandra looked away and stared at the stony portrait of her own mother staring at her from across the way.

The cold eyes that matched her own dark ones drilled into her, as if telling her all she knew about the treacheries lying within Elisandra's cold, cold heart. Her mother had been kind, loving and supportive. What had made things as they are now? Elisandra had challenged her mother for the position as ruler of the Unseelie, but it had not gone the way she'd hoped. Her mother, Queen Analise had watched her daughter approach her throne, throw out the challenging words and had never flinched. She'd stood, taken her sword, which Elisandra had never actually seen her use, and had softly padded down the steps to stand in front of her only daughter.

"I knew this day would come. I am honored to die by the hand of my only daughter. But, do answer me one question before we begin."

Elisandra had stood there, waiting impatiently, ready to impale her mother with a virulent air. How so few words, calm like the eye of storm could disarm her so made her fume at the thought of it now.

"What is it, mother?" Elisandra had spat out, lifting her own sword as she readied to slice it through the body of the one nurturer she'd ever known.

Analise peered at her daughter, sadness finally surfacing in her dark, pretty eyes. The beauty of their line was never surpassed by any Unseelie. They were the untouchable in their looks, where other Unseelie would usually be consumed by the darkness of their kingdom, the rancid evil and treacheries that lingered over them, cursing them to this region of the Land of Faerie, Analise's line had no such affliction. Their beauty was never marred, no matter how defective the soul within had become.

"What will you do when it is your own daughter standing before you as you do now before me?"

Elisandra had taken a step back, shaking at the formidable question her mother had just asked. How dare she assume her daughter would do such a thing to her if she would ever have one. How could she know if that would even happen?

"I'll never have children. I'll rule forever."

Analise laughed. Her throaty defiance rang across the throne room, vibrating the place with its crisp sureness. It only angered Elisandra to be spited so by her own mother, but she waited, willing her fingers from tightening their grip on the sword and swinging it across her mother's chest.

"You're a fool to believe such things." Analise ceased her laugh and inched forward, never lifting her weapon. "One day, you will have a daughter, one with hair as dark as the raven's feathers, and a soul that will end up much darker than yours. You'll never see it coming. You'll torment her, but she'll never break. You're the fool if you think this is the end of it all. No, she will haunt you from the moment she's born until she cuts you down with her own magic and leaves you to wither and rot, just as you've done to me."

With that Elisandra roared to life, lifting her sword and swinging it toward her mother. Analise met it with the sword she carried, her sadness gone. Her love, gone. Everything between them faded with one millisecond of betrayal and it stung Elisandra more than she ever could've imagined.

"I'll take your throne, if it's the last thing I do." Elisandra hissed. Her unfounded hatred coursed through her veins, and she herself feared what she would do with it.

"You'll never be the true Queen of the Unseelie. The ruler is chosen, not made. You are not the chosen. You're nothing but an imposter." With that Analise stepped forward, dropping her blade as she allowed Elisandra to sink her sword into her chest.

Elisandra was shocked at the ease of it all, along with a collective gasp throughout the throne room as the watchers whispered amongst themselves at the exchange of power. With that, the swirl of energy claiming the downed royal as queen left her as her body began to crystalize and wither away to nothing but ash. It then hurled itself into Elisandra, coursing through her veins and slamming its power into her soul.

It was disorientating, especially since it had not been done willingly. The power found her distasteful and protested as it bonded with her being. This forced unity made her sick and she fell to her knees, feeling the rush like a nauseating whoosh. Once it was done fusing, the silence surrounding her made her feel suddenly very much alone.

And she would be, and would remain so for several hundreds of years.

Chapter Seven

Aveta sat on the balcony of her room. The Withering Palace stood high above the ground, on the edge of a treacherous mountain that surveyed the lands beyond the Unseelie borders. The black taint darkened the trees here, kept a constant gloom hovering over the castle and land as if it was a funnel of black smog like the cities of humans had. But it wasn't smog. It was the evil power, which left a sort of scar on the land, marring its beauty, marking it as the territory of the impure.

Aveta didn't see herself as impure. She wondered why the Land of Faerie would be so prejudice and hold such things against her people. They did rage war a lot, but that was Elisandra's doing. With the amount of land they had acquired from the Seelie, Aveta would be mighty content to rule it for a very long time. Maybe it was different after ruling for so long. Maybe after a while, it got boring and a ruler had to amass even more to stay happy. What then? What then when she grew tired of all which had been obtained? Would she change? Would her soul darken into a withered echo of itself, much like her mother's had?

She hoped not. Pushing the thick braid of her hair over her shoulder, she cherished the sunset, a rich gold and peach color that reminded her of the poppy fields with

Cranston. It'd been three years since she'd seen him. She had been confined to her chambers by her mother for unknown reasons three years ago upon returning from the fields beneath the Withering Palace.

Locked in a tower, alone.

This had made her bitter, angry and lonely. Elisandra's time was coming fast. Aveta knew this better than anyone else.

Even Eladril had been forbidden to see her. No one came in, no one left. Her meals would appear out of thin air, probably casted into being by Elisandra from the other side. No servants to clean up or help Aveta into her clothes. The place would be magically perfect when she'd awaken in the mornings, no matter how trashed she'd let it become. It was enchanted. A bubble of purity that left her an immaculate prison. No escape, no interactions.

How long could she tolerate this without going mad?

*****

Cranston sat and studied the tiny entrance to the cavern from which Aveta would always emerge. It'd been far too long. Surely she'd died? He couldn't be sure in any which way what had happened to her. All he knew was that entering the cavern would bring certain death in a vast labyrinth made of dark, withered things. If he could survive it, maybe he could find her. But he remained here, on the other side of the wall that held his beloved from him.

She was alive. He knew it. There would be no separating them for he loved her with all of his being and knew he would feel it if she'd died.

That cursed queen! How dare she keep them apart like this? He was sure she had something to do with it, but wasn't sure. What could he do to stop it? He was but a farm boy from an uncharted Faerie territory, surely his powers were nothing compared to that of the dark queen's?

He picked another petal of poppy flower and rolled it in between his fingers, letting the juice stain his fingertips with its scent. The tiny fluid that emerged was poisonous, but he, his family and Aveta were immune to it. He could poison the queen somehow. That could work.

The labyrinth. It was still the first obstacle and he had no idea how to get through it like Aveta did. She was different, powerful, and strong. He was nothing to compare himself to her. There would be nothing but death for him if he entered the labyrinth.

So he waited and stared day after day at the darkened entrance, his heart breaking ever so slightly as the days, months, years went by. Aveta needed him, but he was trapped here, with no recourse on how to fix this. He'd wait forever for her to return, and she would return. He knew that was the only certainty of this life.

Chapter Eight

Elisandra looked at the rising sun, searing her eyes as it rose over the eastern mountains. This day was tainted; she could feel it in her bones and down her spine. Something was going to happen today, but she could not put her finger on it, no matter how hard she tried to meditate and listen to the powers of the land around her. They shunned her, like the royal power had done so long ago. It still writhed with her, driving her mad after centuries of fighting it. Was her time near? Could that be what it was trying to tell her?

No. it could not be. She'd made sure Aveta was imprisoned forever in her chambers, never allowed to leave. She'd make sure that girl would rot and wither in her room, never to be queen. So what else could it be? What was bothering her so on this cold November day?

Walking through the hallways, she rushed down the darkened corridors, past the main ballroom, and down the steps to the soldier's quarters, and right past that to the dungeons. Here, she stood, a gathering of her guards behind her, ready to pummel any soldier who got out of line. Nothing was down here but a retched stench and derelicts being tortured for all eternity. She briefly flicked her eyes into the cells and wondered if any of them had anything to tell. Most were lost in their own minds, maddened by the constant barrage of pain and tormented curses that'd been thrown onto them for endless deprivation.

Her eyes landed on one figure, sitting near the edge of the

bars to his cell. His long hair covered his face and the filth stuck to his skin like it had embedded itself into it. He didn't look her way, but she could feel his consciousness listening to her. He would do. He was the closest to alive that this place could produce right now.

"You," she approached the bars and stared at him as he refused to look up. With that, she motioned some of her guards forward to grab him. They entered his cell and jerked him to his feet. He groaned and shoved back, chains raddling back against the bars as he sucker punched one of the guards, sending him flying to the ground and stilled.

"Stop!" She commanded, sending a rush of magic to stall him in his movements. He yelped and crumbled to the ground grabbing at his stomach as she twisted it with her magic. "You will answer to me anything I ask you, understand?"

He nodded and let out a breath of air as she released him. He huffed, gasping to catch up breathing as he turned his head into the bars and stared out at the Unseelie Queen.

"Now, tell me, how long have you been here?"

He spat on the ground and cleared his throat, never removing his glare from the Queen. "I've been here ten years."

Another yelp as the guard next to him kicked his side. "You will address the Queen as 'Your Majesty', Seelie scum."

Elisandra held her hand up, motioning the guard to stop. "Now, tell me. Have you ever seen the princess down here?"

The prisoner rubbed at his side, the chains rattled louder as they clanked against one another. "Yes, Your Majesty. I've seen her many times walking down here, though she has not been here for a very long time."

"How long ago did you first see her down here?"

"I—I believe not long after I became a prisoner here, ten years or so."

"Did you know where she went that day?"

He nodded, looking curiously at the queen and up to her soldiers with disdain. "I believe she was headed toward the labyrinth. Though she'd always come back. No one survives that thing, so I heard."

Elisandra rubbed her fingers together, turning down the long hall to the end, where the cavern to the labyrinth stood. The hairs on her back stood up like static and her fear ebbed up toward her throat, choking her breath off. Why would the girl go toward the labyrinth? She would surely die. Maybe she went to the entrance and never entered. Yes, she wouldn't be so stupid would she?

"Very well. Anything else you noticed strange down here?"

The prisoner stared at the queen, feeling the pressure of her power pressing against him. He was stripped of his powers, but he could still shield her from his deepest thoughts if he fought hard enough. And this he did, for the beautiful Eladril had always brought him some food down here in this pestilence of a place. He would never give her up, even if it meant death.

"No, Your Majesty. Nothing unusual besides a little girl playing about."

Elisandra kept her gaze firmly on his, never relenting as she probed at his mind. It made him wince at the pressure, but he did not collapse under it. After a few minutes of this, Elisandra let out a long sigh, waving her guards to drag the unconscious guard out of the cell and locked the prisoner back up.

As they walked away, the prisoner watched with lucid eyes as the Queen disappeared down the way. Leaning his back against the wall, he closed his eyes, exhausted from the invasion and tired of fighting. One day he would wither, if they let him, for the chains that bound him forbade him such a pleasure, to join the afterlife. Maybe, just maybe, one day he would find his way back home and out to the poppy fields again, where his son was surely a man now and the woman who held his heart probably still awaited him.

Chapter Nine

Aveta focused on the shield, sending another jolt rumbling through the barrier in hopes of destroying it. Another pulse, the shield still standing as it had before, easily absorbing the power hurled at it. No changes, not even a crack.

She groaned and threw her hands down. Angry that her powers, however different they may be, couldn't penetrate the shield, leaving her effectively imprisoned here. What could she do? Would she be stuck here forever? Even Eladril was no longer able to visit her. This angered her, for she was restless and fraught with loneliness. She felt like she was going mad. She would make her mother pay for this…for everything.

If she could only get out of this place. She would then have a fighting chance to challenge the Queen for position of power.

But was she ready to end her mother's life? She sank down onto her bed, rocking herself back and forth as the minutes ticked on by. She loathed her mother, yes. But she didn't want to see her dead. It was so final, so unforgiveable it made her blood run cold. It would be the end of innocence for her, the end of everything a young Aveta was made of.

It would mean the start of the new Aveta, hard and unforgiving. Unrelenting as a ruler of the Unseelie Kingdom should be. And what of love? What of Cranston? She'd spent her days daydreaming of seeing him, hearing his voice, touching his skin and holding his hands. How many hours had she laid there on this very bed and wondered how he was doing, what he thought might've happened to her. What if he'd felt betrayed because she had not visited in so long? What if he no longer cared for her? And what, Faerie forbid, what if he had moved on already?

She shook her head, shaking off the dread with one final swoop. She couldn't let the darkness win. She had to keep the hope alive that he remembered her and knew she would eventually return. One day, she would see Cranston again.

With that she stood, walking to the barrier and taking a good hard look through the drying tears in her eyes. She pulled her dark inky black hair away from her pale face and tied it with a leather string. Cracking her knuckles she stood tall and closed her eyes, feeling with nothing more than her senses, the world outside the barrier.

"Withering Palace, hear my call and come to my aid. I know you hear me, my trusted companion. Please help me, for I am in need of your assistance. I am trapped, prisoner within your walls. I know you would not allow this if you could hear me. I know you would let me go for this is your domain and only your power supersedes the ruler of this realm. Please…help me right the powers of the Land of Faerie and grant me justice. Let me go."

A pop distracted her and the walls began to shake. She stepped back and spun around to see that the room was morphing into something else. The wall against the fireplace crumbled, revealing a door behind where the fireplace had been. Her mouth hung open for she'd never known the door existed behind there. How could she not have known? The Withering Palace had never mentioned it to her either. It was unsettling to know the palace held more secrets than she could ever have in a lifetime.

Working past the shock, she stepped forward, reached for the door and turned the ancient knob. It creaked opened and rained down a shower of dust and cobwebs onto the princess. She coughed and swiped at the muck as fast as she could. She wasn't a fan of spiders, but they were tolerable. Of that she was glad as she entered the darkness beyond. As she cleared the door, it slammed behind her in an ominous thud. She shook at the fear pulsating through her now, but crept forward as ancient light torches flared to life before her, and she made her way further and further down the slope.

What would be at the end of this hall? She didn't have long to wonder, though it descended deeper and deeper into the guts of the castle, she began to wonder if it was leading her to the very place she wanted to be—the poppy fields.

The hall began to straighten and then another door appeared, laden with cobwebs and unused for what looked like centuries. She smiled as she swiped them away and turned the knob, excited to get out of her room for the first time in three years.

The door revealed the cavern, the very one she had treaded through many times. As she stepped into it, the door behind creaked shut, but not loudly as the other had. She stared back at it and wondered if it would open for her again. It didn't matter though. She would not go willingly to her prison again.

With that she turned into the cavern, stepping out of it for a moment to get her bearings. The long hall of cells greeted her as before, where prisoners of long term confinement laid and could barely lift their heads to acknowledge her. For some reason, the cells called to her. She stepped forward when one of the torches next to the cell on her right flared to life.

The Withering Palace wanted her to do something, she knew it did. Though its whispers had been silent with the infernal barrier around her room, she could slowly hear them chanting their malevolent banter and get louder as she approached the cell.

The man laid against the bars, weakened and in dire need of nourishment. His clothes were in rags on his body and the filth clung to him like a film. She wrinkled her nose at the stench, but remembered that this man had to be freed. She stared at the lock and reached for it and gasped as it clicked open and the door slipped open by itself.

Take him home, take him to Cranston.

Aveta jumped at the voice so clear and crisp in her head. The Withering Palace was desperate for her to hurry and she did, running into the cell and pulling at the prisoner.

"Come on, we have to go." The prisoner moaned and took some coaxing until he did look up, crisp blue eyes like a bright summer day stared back at her. She paused, transfixed on those eyes. They looked exactly like someone she knew. She had to scan her memory for the right person, but they matched exactly, to her utter surprise.

"Cranston?"

The person stared at her and smiled, but shook his head. Under the grit and film of dirt that clung to his beard and marred his face, she could see a very distinct resemblance.

"No, but we met once. Long ago."

She scanned her memory, wondering where they could've met. If he was Cranston's relation, he reminded her of…his father?

"Your Cranston's father." She could not recall his name, but the smile blooming on this stranger's face confirmed enough for her. "Come on, we need to go now. Can you walk?"

"Slowly, but yes. I've not eaten for weeks." She slipped her arm around his waist, slipping his arm over her shoulders. She wasn't super strong, but strong enough with the continued sword practice she would do in her room by herself. That was one thing a Faerie Royal was always taught, sword fighting and weapons knowledge. It was the one thing keeping her strong now.

The smell was atrocious, but she bit her lip and pressed on, nearly dragging him out of the cell and into the small cavern that aligned with the entrance of the Labyrinth.

"We don't have much time."

"I won't survive the cavern again." He mumbled.

She groaned, staring at the foreboding darkness ahead.

"You won't have to, I can get through quickly, and I know all the shortcuts. You'll have to keep your eyes closed, the entire way, no matter what you hear. Understand?"

He nodded and limped along with her until the entrance of the cavern, where he cringed and shut his eyes.

"Ready?" Aveta heard the guards yelling behind her and they jumped into the doorway behind her as she readied to step through the threshold and into the inky darkness of the Labyrinth, where the soldiers did not follow.

The trek through the Labyrinth was short, but still took a lot out of Aveta as she dragged the man along with her. She pulled and tugged, and through the screeches of the wraith's and darklings within, they limped along. She could ignore them, but many times the man screamed in horror as things grasped at him or called his name. She could've called up the stone statues, but her power had to be reserved for healing if she was to help this man.

"Ignore them." How long it'd been since she had trudged

through here, yet she was as confident as ever and kept strong to the short trail she'd found through the massive rock labyrinth.

The man tripped, sending them both to the floor, into a puddle of water, collected surely from the recent rainfall. Aveta scurried to lift him back to his feet, but the water made him slippery and she struggled to gain a grip on him.

"Come on, you need to get on your feet." She felt the creatures building around them, watching, waiting to be acknowledged, but she refused. "Come on, Cranston is waiting for us."

The man struggled to his feet, keeping his eyes pressed together and took her embrace for assistance. They were both filthy now and the mud stuck to her dress like a formidable grit. She carried on, having lost a shoe in the mud.

"Almost there."

"Thank you." He whispered, sounding close to exhaustion as they finally made it through the labyrinth and Aveta breathed a sigh of relief as they stepped into the light of the opening to the poppy fields.

It was a sight for sore eyes and she felt the tears streaming down her dirty cheeks as they limped on, slipping down onto the poppy flowers, where the red dirt beneath them stained their clothes and fingers and the poppies powdered them in a welcoming puff.

"Cranston!" She yelled, her voice echoed in the desolate field and she hoped he could hear her now. "Please," Aveta pulled herself up to stand and spun, searching the field for him. The cherry blossoms swayed, silent and unknowing of their plight. "Cranston! Help us!"

Chapter Ten

Cranston washed his hands, full of grit, old blood and other unmentionables. Aveta sat on the meager kitchen table, dressed in one of his sister's dresses. Her hair was neatly brushed, but still soaked from the recent scrubbing she'd given herself. Cranston's cottage was small, but quaint, and it felt oddly more like home than any place she'd ever been.

She stared at the bottom of her mug, watching the remains of her tea swish around, wondering how things had gotten so bad. She was happy she had made back into the safety of the poppy fields and Cranston's arms. He was relieved to find her, but the fear that he was hallucinating immediately turned to fear for his father, Ceric. His father had disappeared ten years before, after Aveta had arrived to the poppy fields. No one knew what had happened to him or where he'd gone off to. All they knew that he was here one moment and gone the next.

No one asked Ceric what had happened that long ago day, or how he'd entered the Unseelie world only to end up in the dungeon. No, there would be time for that later, when things were more settled and Aveta had taken care of Queen Elisandra. It'd be the only way any of them could live in peace.

"Thank you," Cranston sat across from her and slipped his hands into hers. He'd changed some since she last saw him, he was huskier, thicker and his face had lost any baby fat he'd had from his growing years. They'd both reached their maturity and now appeared as they would for all eternity, for as long as they remained alive. Faeries were immortal, though many did not make it past three to five hundred years. The years caught up to many of them and they chose to wither instead, a chosen death where the faery would start to waste away until one day, they turned to ash and returned to the earth.

"The Withering Palace, the voices it speaks to me with…they took me to your father, to help him. Had I known he was there sooner, I would've helped, you must know that…" Her voice shook and she stared hard down at her mug, afraid to look up.

"It's all right. You didn't know he was there. I'm thankful beyond words that you even found him and brought him back alive. I know what an impossible task it is to make it through the labyrinth, especially with someone as weak as my father. The labyrinth is malicious, but it also keeps our world safe from the Unseelie."

"Do you think they'll come through?"

Cranston shook his head, softly running circles across her skin with his fingertips. It sent shivers up her spine and deep into her chest. "No. They have never come here, ever. I don't think they will now."

Aveta nodded, turning her cold mug around in her palms. It wasn't very reassuring, but she knew it was true. All good things must be equaled with evil, hence the existence of the Unseelie in the first place. She sighed, closing her eyes and wishing it wasn't her life, that it wasn't her position to assume command of such a daunting task.

But it was her duty. It was her life to lead and nothing would ever change that. Not even her love for Cranston.

She stood up, taking her mug to the sink and dumping it there before turning toward Cranston. The somber look on his face told her everything she wanted to know, and it hurt to have to leave him again so soon.

"Must you leave already?" He reached out and slipped his hands over her hips to pull her closer. She let him, unable to resist being near him.

"I'm sorry. I have to go, there's something I have to finish."

Cranston gave her a tiny nod, leaning forward and touched forehead to forehead with her. She sighed, letting his woodsy, poppy flower scent fill her nose. It was calming, like a sedative wanting to seduce her in and never let her go. She had to let go, even if she didn't want to. If there was ever a moment she didn't want to end, this was it.

"Don't forget me."

"Never."

He pulled back, planting a kiss on her head. Gazing straight into each other's eyes for minutes, Aveta relished his strong arms encircling her and his handsome face.

"I've waited a long time for you, my love. I'll wait forever more."

Aveta smiled, tears glistening on her dark eyes. "And I for you."

With that, he bent down and kissed her lips, softly at first, then a deep, wanting kiss that sped both their hearts up and left them breathless. Aveta pulled away before she could change her mind, touched her lips, feeling the warmth of his still dancing across them.

"I love you. I'll be back."

"I love you, too," he nodded, and followed her to the door where he watched her cross the road and tread into the poppy fields to the oppressive mountain ahead, where the cavern to the Labyrinth was. Something told him he might never see her again, so he continued to watch her until her figure disappeared into the horizon and could no longer be seen.

Even then, he remained studying the spot she had last been. The poppies swayed with the slight breeze, dark pink under the burnt orange sky. How many days, weeks or months would he stare over this part of the fields until she returned? How much time would go by this time before he was graced with her beautiful face once more? He wasn't sure, but something told him, it would be an eternity.

Chapter Eleven

Elisandra rushed forward, shoving her soldiers to the side as she passed through the dungeon and to the end to where the cavern to the Labyrinth began. She studied the dark hole in the wall, ominous and never disturbed by the dungeon guards or any Unseelie, for they knew what laid beyond. Nothing but death awaited them in the blackness.

"Where is she?" The Queen's rage flushed her face scarlet and her disgust at being down here in the pits of the Withering Palace made her even more maddened. "Where did that little wench of a daughter of mine go? How did she escape?"

The first soldier, her Second Lieutenant, stood straight to answer her as her soldiers cowered behind him. He was a tall man, thin, but also a muscular faery. He'd kept the ranks well trained and ready at a moment's notice to invade any place she so wished to conquer. He was not expendable as she would've liked, but that didn't mean the men behind him, shaking in their britches, weren't.

"We are uncertain to how she escaped, possibly a secret tunnel, but we know it led her here, where she helped in the escape of a known fugitive and took him into the Labyrinth, Your Majesty."

"So why has she not been pursued?" She drilled her stare into her Second Lieutenant, waiting for him to crack. But the top soldiers were conditioned to not break and he merely looked down, a show of inferiority to the Queen. Not a lick of fear graced his face, and this angered her even more.

A crack sounded as she sent out her magic to the soldier beside her lieutenant, zapping the poor soul until he crumbled to their feet, nothing but soot and smoldering ashes.

"Find her." She hissed before she turned back toward the cavern entrance as the girl, Aveta, passed into the room from the darkness.

"I'm here now, mother." Aveta stood in peasant rags, looking even younger than her eighteen years.

Elisandra stormed forward about to grab the girl when the same loud crack sounded and she was sent crumbling to her knees. Aveta had used her elemental power to shake the ground under Elisandra's feet and made her lose her balance. How dare she?

"What have you done? You dare challenge your own mother?"

Aveta stared hard at the woman as she regained her footing and glared back with only hatred exuding from every pore of her body.

"No, I see no mother here. I see the Unseelie Queen, unfit to rule. I challenge you for the throne as due to me, rightfully by blood and as chosen of the Withering Palace."

Aveta stepped forward, but the queen did not move.

"You fool. You don't know what you're doing. There is no going back from this."

Aveta tilted her head, her face an ocean of calm and determination. "I know."

Elisandra narrowed her eyes as her soldiers backed away to the required distance for the two to dual. Aveta didn't even have a sword so she motioned her lieutenants to hand her one and grabbed her own from a servant holding it out to her.

"This shouldn't take too long, princess. You've grown soft in your years of confinement."

How sure the queen seemed. How naïve she'd become in the years since she'd seen her daughter. Aveta was now taller than her, thin and lean, but strong. Her feet were bare, but that did not hinder her stance as she prepared to fight to the end.

"No softer than your heart will ever be, mother." With that Elisandra lurched forward and swung her sword, only to meet Aveta's in a stand still, she pushed away and swung again, then again and again. Each time Aveta matched her, and they remained stalled. With that, she shoved at her daughter and stood back, breathing harder with nothing but evil marring her beauty.

"Seems you've kept up your fighting studies. Very well, disarm her. It will be a battle of magic and wits then. Give in now, before this meets you with your death." She threw her sword down and Aveta did the same, servants reached in and pulled the metal away and backed into the thick of the crowd once more. A challenge was taken seriously in Faerie, especially for the throne. There would be no treachery, for the land of Faerie would not allow it. It was fight to the death or until one gave in. Usually, it was death, for faeries were honorable things who held such a disgust for failure.

Elisandra launched first, a swirling, black funnel meant to blow Aveta backward into the rock wall, but Aveta matched it with a counter wind that caused it to die into stillness. Immediately, the Queen expelled out spikes of rock flying toward the girl with a deathly velocity. Aveta dodged one, but one managed to slice across her thigh. She let out a scream as she rolled onto the ground, scraping her knees and elbows. She didn't stay down long. She jumped to her feet before Elisandra sent a storm of fire balls smacking into the ground around her.

Aveta tossed a storm of rocks toward the fireballs, blocking most of them with a rain of sparks. With that she backed up in to the entrance to the cavern, already feeling some exhaustion from dodging all the magical objects sent her way.

"Coward! How dare you run?"

"I do not run, mother. I challenge you to catch me if you can, in the Labyrinth." With that she was swallowed by the inky blackness of the cavern, her soft laugh echoed behind her as she waited for her mother to follow into the abyss of madness.

Elisandra stood at the entrance, appalled that she had to follow into the Labyrinth. It was a challenge and in no way could she not continue. She cursed under her breath and peered behind her.

"If she comes out, kill her."

No one nodded, not even her lieutenants, who knew full well that if the princess emerged and the Queen did not, they would not be killing her.

"You fools," Elisandra hissed and ignited a torch she formed in her hand as she entered the black oblivion of the

Labyrinth.

Inside, it was the darkest night that she had ever seen and the corridors made her feel claustrophobic. Her steps echoed as they crunched over pebbles and sand across the stone floor. Still, there was nothing, no sign of Aveta, no creatures that were supposed to leach her life force away. Nothing approached and she relaxed as the minutes ticked on by and she headed further and further into the darkness.

"Where are you, sweet daughter…" Her madness seeped into her buoyant words and her tiny cackles echoed across the chambers. "You'll never survive this. You'll die before you get out of this empty place."

A rush of wind and Aveta slammed into her, sending the torch flying to the ground. With that, Aveta ran off again into the obsidian darkness.

"How dare you!" Elisandra gritted as she pulled her twisted ankle out from under her, whispering healing charm over it as it swelled and purpled in color. "Stupid heathen. I'll kill her." Her ankle began to mend itself, but it had left her shaken. How dare her daughter do this to her? How dare she not just give up and die like she should've the day she was born.

She regretted having the girl. She'd only had her at the insistence of her husband Seritus, her first lieutenant. She loved him once, enough to give him such a gift, but no longer. Eventually, she'd casted him aside like an unwanted lover. He remained though, always faithful to her, always trustworthy. He'd never been involved in raising the girl after that, which had fractured his soul like fallen ice. It was his punishment for wanting her to bear him a child. Now, that mistake was making Elisandra pay in another way. If only she'd drowned the infant when she should've. Instead, she had tossed the girl into the care of Eladril, who had cared for and loved the girl so well, she'd become a full-fledged force to deal with.

Oh, how full of regret Elisandra was filled with now. So many errors in such a powerful life. It had left her colder and void of any love, a fractured soul within herself, withering without her knowledge.

She hopped onto her feet, her ankle still tender, but healing. Dusting off her long swathes of fabric that made up her dress, she stepped forward, wincing from the continued ache in her leg, but it lessened as time went on. With that, she fashioned a dagger from the stones around her and waited for another surprise attack. This time she'd be ready. This time, Aveta would not leave unscathed.

"Elisandra?" The Queen stopped in her tracks, paling at the sight of her own mother, looking young and vibrant as she had the day she had struck her down.

"Mother?"

"My sweet daughter. How long it's been."

Elisandra couldn't move, frozen in her spot as she stared at the figure of her mother, Analise, stepping forward and slowly reaching her arms out.

"My Elsi. Why have you left me here to wither? How could you turn your back on me?"

Elisandra shook her head, stepping back, no longer feeling the searing pain in her ankle but a paralyzing fear enveloping her chest, making hard to breathe. "No, I never left you here. You're dead. I—I killed you! I took the throne. It's MINE!" She stepped back again, but her mother did not stop or fade. In fact each moment Elisandra believed her to be there, the stronger her figure became, no longer translucent, but solid and fleshed out.

"Elsi, you have to help me. You must get me out of here, for I am trapped, damned for all eternity…"

Elisandra lowered her dagger, her mouth dropping open at her mother's words. "What do you mean? You're dead. How can you be here? I never damned you. I sent you to the Summerlands, where it's warm and quiet, away from here."

Her mother smiled, pity blossoming in her face before she shook her head. "No, my dear child. I am lost, lost here forever because you damned me to this. Now, help me."

Elisandra didn't know what to do as the figure approached. So like her mother, so much so that she believed the wraith to be her. She looked so real, so much like the mother who had loved her and held her when the nightmares came, deep into the night. The same mother who'd soothe her when her magic would not cooperate and she had to do her lessons over and over again. The same loving mother who had tucked her into bed at night until… until…

Her mother had decided Elisandra, her daughter, was a

threat. She had assassins sent to kill her one night as she slept. Her mother had lost her mind and had begun seeing things. She had penned Elisandra as another conspirator who had replaced her daughter and wanted her offed. Just like that, without confirming that it was really Elisandra whom she had ordered to end.

"No, don't touch me! Don't touch…" But her breath was cut off and she gasped as a blade jutted out from her chest, brilliant and bloody all at the same time.

"Don't you know, mother? Don't you know to never give a wraith the power to own you? It's not hard, really." Aveta shoved the knife further in and let her go, Elisandra crumbled to the floor, writhing and gasping for air.

Aveta watched her, knowing the wraith who had entranced her mother was near. She paid it no mind and without Elisandra to feed it, it faded and disappeared once more. Aveta did not smile or relish in the death of her mother. Though Elisandra still gasped and was unable to heal herself with the knife embedded in her heart, Aveta felt nothing. In fact, she felt so empty inside, and she knew it would be awhile before she felt anything again.

"Aveta…" Elisandra gasped as she reached toward her daughter, but the young woman stepped away.

"You stole me from my love. You chained me to my chambers without company, without a visit or a second thought of me. You threw me away and I did nothing but love you." Aveta spoke, but the words seem to come from someone else as she stared at her mother, who still struggled to breathe. The Queen shook her head, tears streaming down her face.

"Traitorous child…"

"Am I?" Aveta bent down to look at her mother eye to eye. "But who is the queen now?"

Elisandra's face morphed to cold fury as she watched her daughter straighten and turn to leave the labyrinth.

"I have one thing left to take." Elisandra hissed.

Aveta paid no mind as she continued her walk down the cavernous hall.

"You said I took your love from you? No. I did no such thing. But…I will make that accusation real. This one last moment, I grant you this one last thing."

Aveta's eyes widened and she turned to find the Queen holding her hands up in the air and whispering a curse as she closed her eyes and shot the last of her magic up toward the roof of the cavern.

What was she doing?

Aveta felt the ground rumble and swayed, reaching out to catch herself on the cavern wall. As she braced herself, she watched as the wall before her cracked from the ceiling to the ground. All around her, boulders and chunks of the cavern fell, and covered the floor with debris. As moments passed, it got worse as the structure began to collapse and the labyrinth walls began to fall, one by one, bringing much of the ceiling down with them.

Aveta turned to run, down the long corridors, twists and turns she'd memorized so many years ago. She dodged walls tilting down on her and shards of stalactites falling from nowhere and stabbing the ground with their massive spikes. She ran until the end of the cavern appeared, the one to the dungeon. As she turned back, she saw the last of the cavern disintegrate into rubble, impenetrable and full of boulders and rocks taller than any man.

She barely jumped into the dungeon when the cavern entrance sealed itself off from the rest of the castle with one huge slam of boulders that stopped pouring into the dungeon, as if cut off by some mystical boundary. The dust and dirt puffed into the room and the soldiers coughed and covered their noses as the cloud settled.

Aveta found herself on the ground, dirty, scraped in a trillion spots and her hair in wild tangles. She pushed off the floor to hop onto her feet and stare in horror at the collapsed tunnel which had held entrance to the labyrinth and to her love, Cranston.

"No!" She jumped onto the pile and ordered the stones to move, but only the small boulders dared to move, the larger ones ignored her commands and stayed put. There was no moving them, as if they were meant to seal off the labyrinth forever if they ever collapsed.

"No, please, no!" She slammed her fists against the rock, shaking some loose that rolled onto the ground before her.

"Your Majesty, we should leave, before the rest of the room collapses." Her father, the first lieutenant held his hand out to her as he kneeled before her and touched her back gently.

His voice echoed in her head, but she barely registered it. She allowed him to lead her out of the dungeon and up into the rest of the Withering Palace. The soldiers and sluagh alike all kneeled as she walked past, a Queen in rags, dirty and bloodied from war. She had won everything and lost everything at the same time. A bitter sweet taste to relish.

He led her to Eladril, who'd also been enchanted to stay in her quarters for the last three years, but the spell was broken now and her faithful servant emerged, knowing without even asking what had ensued. She led the new Queen to her chambers to heal her, clean her up and redress her as the royal leader of all the Unseelie.

It was a glorious day for all as Queen Aveta ascended to her throne, a chair she had observed her entire life with wonder, now it held nothing but hate and heartbreak. She would never be happy here, but she had to rule, that was the whole idea of it all in the first place.

The only comfort she took in everything was that Cranston and his family were safe, deep beyond the dungeons of The Withering Palace in a place where poppies grew under the cherry blossom trees and the wind smelled of sweet honey, destined to remain peaceful forever. No one would bother them, as long as she lived, she would make sure no one knew of that place, a secret realm of Faerie.

Only The Withering Palace was privy to such a thing, and it spoke to no one but Aveta.

The End

Acknowledgements:

I want to thank my Indie Inked sisters. Your support has been endless and has pushed me to my limits, which I thought I'd never reach. I love you guys and I know you'll always have my back, and I yours.

Special thanks to my personal assistant Doris Orman, whose endless support has helped me become a better writer by freeing me up to do more of it. You rock and I'm lost without you!

Special thanks to those who helped me with some last minute stuff: Donna Gardner, J.T. Lewis, Joy Whiteside, Tiffany Saylor, Michelle McQueen, Raven Williams, Amber Wright, Juniper Wadsworth Olsen, Kathy Hanners, Sherry Christenson, Mira Dei Medici, Jennifer Martinez, Meredith Huyck and, Sandy Marie Apeldoorn,

Finally, thank you to my readers, you rock in every sense of the word. Your endless support help me continue doing what I love, telling stories! Without you, I'd still be lost in my own head by myself. Thank you!

About the Author

Alexia currently lives in Las Vegas, Nevada—Sin City! She loves to spend every free moment writing or playing with her four rambunctious kids. Writing has always been her dream, and she has been writing ever since she can remember. She loves writing paranormal fantasy and poetry and devours books daily. Alexia also enjoys watching movies, dancing, singing loudly in the car and eating Italian food.

Please follow Alexia Purdy's Newsletter for exclusive content, freebies, giveaways and more!

Also by Alexia Purdy:

9 781501 015489